Teggs is no ordinary dinosaur –
he's an **ASTROSAUR!** Captain of
the amazing spaceship DSS *Sauropod*,
he goes on dangerous missions and
fights evil – along with his faithful
crew, Gipsy, Arx and Iggy.

For more astro-fun visit the website
www.astrosaurs.co.uk

Read all the adventures of
Teggs, Gipsy, Arx and Iggy!

RIDDLE OF THE RAPTORS
THE HATCHING HORROR
THE SEAS OF DOOM
THE MIND-SWAP MENACE
THE SKIES OF FEAR
THE SPACE GHOSTS
DAY OF THE DINO-DROIDS
THE TERROR-BIRD TRAP
THE STAR PIRATES
THE CLAWS OF CHRISTMAS
THE SUN-SNATCHERS
REVENGE OF THE FANG
THE CARNIVORE CURSE
THE DREAMS OF DREAD

Read all the adventures of Teggs, Blink
and Dutch at Astrosaurs Academy!

DESTINATION DANGER!
CONTEST CARNAGE!
TERROR UNDERGROUND!
JUNGLE HORROR!
Coming soon!
DEADLY DRAMA!

Find out more at www.astrosaurs.co.uk

Astrosaurs

THE DREAMS OF DREAD

Steve Cole

Illustrated by Woody Fox

RED FOX

THE DREAMS OF DREAD
A RED FOX BOOK 978 1 862 30545 8

First published in Great Britain by Red Fox,
an imprint of Random House Children's Books
A Random House Group Company

This edition published 2009

1 3 5 7 9 10 8 6 4 2

Text copyright © Steve Cole, 2009
Cover illustration and cards © Dynamo Design, 2009
Map © Charlie Fowkes, 2009
Illustrations copyright © Woody Fox, 2009

Typeset in Bembo MT Schoolbook 16/20pt
by Falcon Oast Graphic Art Ltd.

Red Fox Books are published by Random House Children's Books,
61–63 Uxbridge Road, London W5 5SA

www.kidsatrandomhouse.co.uk
www.rbooks.co.uk

Addresses for companies within The Random House Group Limited can
be found at: www.randomhouse.co.uk/offices.htm

THE RANDOM HOUSE GROUP Limited Reg. No. 954009

A CIP catalogue record for this book is available from the British Library.

Printed in the UK by CPI Bookmarque, Croydon, CR0 4TD

For Hector Crosbie – an astro-sir

WARNING!

THINK YOU KNOW ABOUT DINOSAURS?

THINK AGAIN!

The dinosaurs . . .

Big, stupid, lumbering reptiles. Right?

All they did was eat, sleep and roar a bit. Right?

Died out millions of years ago when a big meteor struck the Earth. Right?

Wrong!

The dinosaurs weren't stupid. They may have had small brains, but they used them well. They had big thoughts and big dreams.

By the time the meteor hit, the last dinosaurs had already left Earth for ever. Some breeds had discovered how to travel through space as early as the Triassic period, and were already enjoying a new life among the stars. No one has found evidence of dinosaur technology yet. But the first fossil bones were only unearthed in 1822, and new finds are being made all the time.

The proof is out there, buried in the ground.

And the dinosaurs live on, way out in space, even now. They've settled down in a place they call the Jurassic Quadrant and over the last sixty-five million years they've gone on evolving.

The dinosaurs we'll be meeting are

part of a special group called the Dinosaur Space Service. Their job is to explore space, to go on exciting missions and to fight evil and protect the innocent!

These heroic herbivores are not just dinosaurs.

They are *astrosaurs*!

NOTE: The following story has been translated from secret Dinosaur Space Service records. Earthling dinosaur names are used throughout, although some changes have been made for easy reading. There's even a guide to help you pronounce the dinosaur names on the next page.

Talking Dinosaur!

How to say the prehistoric
names in this book

STEGOSAURUS – STEG-oh-SORE-us

RAPTOR – RAP-tor

PTEROSAUR – teh-roh-SORE

DIMORPHODON – die-MORF-oh-don

TRICERATOPS – try-SERRA-tops

HADROSAUR – HAD-roh-SORE

IGUANODON – ig-WHA-noh-don

ANKYLOSAUR – an-KILE-oh-SORE

THE CREW OF THE DSS SAUROPOD

**CAPTAIN
TEGGS STEGOSAUR**

ARX ORANO,
FIRST OFFICER

GIPSY SAURINE,
COMMUNICATIONS
OFFICER

IGGY TOOTH,
CHIEF ENGINEER

Jurassic Quadrant

Ankylos

Steggos

Diplox

INDEPENDENT
DINOSAUR
ALLIANCE

vegetarian
sector

Squawk
Major

DSS
UNION OF
PLANETS

PTEROSAURIA

Tri System

Corytho

Lambeos

Iguanos

Aqua Minor

Geldos Cluster

Teerex
Major

Olympus

Planet Sixty

TYRANNOSAUR
TERRITORIES

carnivore

sector

Raptos

THEROPOD EMPIRE

Cryptos

Megalos

vegmeat

zone

(neutral space)

SEA REPTILE
SPACE

Pliosaur
Nurseries

Not to scale

THE
DREAMS OF
DREAD

Chapter One

METEOR MENACE

Captain Teggs Stegosaur couldn't sleep.
 The orange-brown stegosaurus lay
in his leafy bed on board the DSS
Sauropod – finest craft in the Dinosaur
Space Service – and sighed. For the last
thirty-six hours, he had been leading his
astrosaur crew through deep space on
a desperate mission to hunt down the
cruellest carnivore in the universe.
 General Loki had escaped from
space prison!

Loki was Teggs's deadliest enemy. They had tangled together three times before. On each occasion it had almost ended in disaster for the peaceful plant-eating dinosaurs of the Vegetarian Sector – and each time, Teggs had barely survived . . .

"How did Loki get out of jail?" Teggs wondered again. No raptor spaceships had been spotted in the area around the prison. And yet something had burned a hole through the super-secure steel walls and snatched Loki away. Experts from DSS HQ had detected a small object in the area heading for the outer reaches of the Jurassic Quadrant, and the *Sauropod* had been sent on its trail.

So far, the crew had found nothing.

"But we can't stop searching. Astrosaurs never give up!" Teggs yawned. "Although they do get slightly sleepy sometimes . . ."

His eyes closed and soon he was dreaming.

The dream began nicely. He was lying on a sunny hillside, chewing on some leafy bushes – Teggs loved eating almost as much as he loved having adventures. But suddenly, the sky darkened and the bushes grew teeth! They snapped at him and rolled closer and closer . . .

Then, an extra-loud explosion made Teggs jump out of bed and bruise his bottom on the floor!

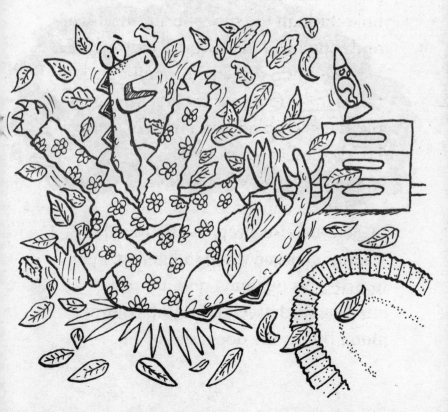

"*Meteor strike!*" The alarm pterosaur's shrill cry echoed over the *Sauropod*'s speakers. "More meteors ahead. Stand by for bumps and thumps. *SQUAWWK!*"

Teggs gasped. Meteors were lumps of rock floating in space, a danger to any passing spaceship. If one of them was to knock a hole in the ship's hull it could be disastrous . . .

"So much for sleep," he muttered. Teggs charged through his ship, still wearing his pyjamas, and jumped into the lift that led up to the control room. But as the doors slid open . . .

"Whoa!" He had to duck down as his
pterosaur flight crew – fifty dazzling
dimorphodon – flapped about, working
the ship's controls with their beaks
and claws.

Through the flurry of dino-birds,
Teggs saw the *Sauropod*'s scanner screen.
It showed the rich blackness of space,
peppered with eerie red sparkles of light.

"Captain!" A green triceratops looked
over from his space radar. This was Arx,
Teggs's brainy second-in-command.
"Sorry to have spoiled your rest."

"That meteor was quite an alarm call!" said Teggs, jumping into his control pit.

Gipsy nodded. She was a stripy hadrosaur who handled the ship's communications, and much more besides. "It put a dent in level seven, even with our shields up."

"Is everyone OK?" Teggs asked anxiously. Not counting the dimorphodon, the *Sauropod* had a crew of fifty dinosaurs on board.

"They're all fine," Arx assured him. "For now, at least!"

"Let's keep them that way," said Teggs. "Reduce our speed to emergency levels." Gipsy whistled to the dimorphodon and they flapped off to obey. Then Teggs turned to Arx. "Can we reverse out of the meteor storm before we're in too deep?"

"We already *are* in too deep, Captain," said Arx gravely. "The storm was all around us in seconds. Hundreds of rocks like bees swarming about a hive."

Gipsy shivered. "Almost as if they were *drawn* to us."

"Perhaps they're magnetic," Teggs suggested.

"No, Captain," said Arx. "I've scanned these space rocks. They are made of a kind of crystal I've never seen before. They seem to contain a strange energy beyond the range of our sensors . . ."

Gipsy gulped. "General Loki might have known about these meteors and lured us here."

Arx nodded. "Or perhaps he's run into trouble with them too."

A tense silence settled on the *Sauropod*'s flight deck as the dimorphodon shifted the ship this way and that, trying to avoid the hurtling meteors. Teggs

chomped on some vines and braced himself for another bone-shaking collision at any moment. But instead, a strange series of soft clangs and rumbles echoed through the ship.

"What's happening?" demanded Teggs.

"I'm not sure," said Gipsy as a loud bleep came from her controls. "But Iggy's just sent a code-two warning signal!"

"That means engine trouble!" Teggs reared up in his pit. "Put him on screen."

Iggy was the *Sauropod*'s Chief Engineer. A stocky iguanodon, he was handy in a fight – and right now he looked ready for one. "Some of those meteors brushed against our jet-thrusters, Captain," he said crossly. "And they're *sticking* there."

"Sticking?" Teggs frowned. "How?"

"I don't know," Arx admitted. "But it could be something to do with that strange energy they each contain . . ."

"Let's try to shake them off," said Teggs.

"Increase speed by ten per cent."

Gipsy whistled again and the dimorphodon flocked into action. But the clatter of wings could not disguise more of the curious clangs, coming thick and fast now.

"Meteors are sticking all over the *Sauropod*," Arx reported.

"They're even blocking our exhaust pipes," groaned Iggy. "If the fuel gases can't get out, they'll keep building up until the engines explode!"

Gipsy's head-crest flushed blue with alarm. "We'll be completely helpless!"

"Arx!" said Teggs urgently, "if we increase our speed, can we blow the meteors out again?"

Arx nodded. "I think it's our only chance."

"Set speed to maximum!" Teggs shouted.

Gipsy whistled, the dimorphodon screeched and the hum of the engines rose in pitch.

"It's working," cried Iggy, and Gipsy cheered. "The meteors are being blasted back into space!"

"They're falling off the rest of the ship too," said Arx excitedly. "But travelling this fast, there's a danger we might—"

CRASSSSSHHHHH!

A massive meteor struck the *Sauropod* like a spoon striking the top of a boiled egg – and with much the same result. Gipsy screamed as the roof caved in. Wreckage rained down over Teggs's control pit, and the dimorphodon were knocked to the ground. Arx was sent staggering into the safety rails.

Teggs looked up through the debris and saw the huge meteor poking through the crumpled roof, smooth as glass and glowing eerily like a massive, crimson night-light. Then a wild wind started up inside the flight deck.

Gipsy gripped her seat. "What's happening?"

"That hole in the roof," Arx gasped, clinging to the safety rail. "Our air's being sucked out into the vacuum of space!"

"Keep holding on!" Teggs shouted. "Or we'll all go with it!"

Chapter Two

THE SUDDEN SLEEP

The air was howling through the hole in the roof. Teggs saw Sprite, the dimorphodon's team leader, flapping for his life as he was dragged remorselessly towards the freezing, deadly blackness beyond.

"Grab hold!" Teggs called, stretching out his spiky tail.

The brave little pterosaur clamped his beak around one of Teggs's spikes. As he did so, he grabbed hold of two of his flapping friends' wings with his talons. Then each of those friends held on to two more friends with *their* talons.

Soon it looked as though Teggs's tail

was flying a living kite of dimorphodon!

Clinging onto her chair with one hoof, Gipsy bashed buttons with the other. "It's no good," she groaned. "Our shields are broken. All the air will drain away."

Arx gulped. "Pretty soon, we won't be able to breathe!"

"Order the rest of the crew to evacuate!" shouted Teggs in desperation. "Perhaps they can escape in the shuttles . . ."

But suddenly, the doors to the flight deck opened – and an iguanodon in a space helmet came somersaulting inside, carrying a large red canister.

"Iggy!" cried Teggs. "Get out of here, it's too dangerous!"

"Just the way I like it," Iggy grinned. He leaped into the air and fired sticky grey foam from his canister all around the weird meteor. As the thick foam filled the cracks in the roof, the howling wind began to hush.

"Emergency super-sealing spray!"
Arx cheered.

"We're airtight again!" Teggs beamed
as Iggy finished filling the holes and the
dimorphodon dropped to the ground
from Teggs's tail in a panting, scaly heap.
"Way to go, Ig!"

Iggy pulled off his helmet and wiped his brow – just in time for Gipsy to plant a big kiss on his snout. "You were brilliant!" she said.

"We're not safe yet." Teggs looked up at the meteor, which looked ready to squash them at any moment. "The *Sauropod* can't survive another crash in this condition. We must make an emergency landing – and start repairing."

Arx checked his space radar. "The only planet in range is a tiny speck in space called Mallakar. No one lives there."

"Then, what are we waiting for?" said Teggs, as Sprite urged the dimorphodon back to their perches. "Let's go there now – very, *very* carefully!"

The astrosaurs breathed more easily once the *Sauropod* was out of the meteor storm. No more of the strange, glassy rocks tried to stick to them. Teggs glanced up at the huge crystal meteor lodged in the battered roof and wondered why . . . What was that weird energy, inside the rocks, *for*?

"There's no sign of life on Mallakar," Arx announced. "Our sensors show that no other spaceship has been here for years."

Iggy listened to the whoosh of the landing jets with great relief. "Wa-hey!" he cried. "We're safely down. For a while there, I thought we were goners!"

Teggs crossed to a porthole and looked outside. The landscape was flat and grey. The only thing of interest was the dark, rocky mouth of a cave, yawning on the barren horizon.

"This is all Loki's fault," said Gipsy, rubbing her eyes. "If he hadn't escaped, we wouldn't be out here looking for him."

"Well, at least we can make sure that the weird meteor storm is added to the DSS star charts," said Teggs. "Then, all other astrosaurs can avoid it."

Arx gazed up at the big red crystal. "I can't wait to study that thing." He yawned noisily. "But maybe first . . . a little rest. I'm feeling really tired – and *you* must be exhausted, Captain."

Teggs nodded sleepily. "It's been a tiring day for us all. Gipsy, broadcast a message to the whole crew – they may take a sleep break."

But Gipsy had already fallen asleep at her controls! So Teggs told everyone over the loudspeakers instead.

Sprite perched on Iggy's head and looked at Teggs. "*Eep!*" he said, his eyes bright and alert.

"Yes," said Teggs, "of course you and your team can start making repairs. But aren't you tired?"

Sprite shook his head. "*Fneep.*"

"Oh! I didn't know that. N'night!" Teggs smiled as he left the flight deck with Iggy and Arx. "I'm glad I took that How-to-Speak-Dimorphodon course!"

It was Iggy's turn to yawn as they climbed into the lift. "What did Sprite say?"

"He said he and his friends weren't feeling sleepy, and he wished us all sweet dreams – but that, actually, flying reptiles don't ever *have* dreams so he doesn't quite know what 'sweet dreams' means."

Iggy frowned. "He said all that with one 'fneep'?"

"It was all in the *way* he said it," Teggs explained with a smile. Then he heard snoring below him — Arx had fallen asleep on the floor of the lift! "I guess our trusty triceratops was more worn out than he realized."

"I am too." Iggy staggered off down the corridor. "Good night, Captain."

Teggs reached his room and collapsed on the bed. Within moments he was fast asleep as well, and dreaming.

He was back on the sunny hillside from his last dream. But this time, it was cold and frosty, despite the sunshine. The belligerent bushes were huddled around him, baring their thorn-like teeth, snapping their jaws like hungry animals . . .

"No!" gasped Teggs, jerking awake from his nightmare.

But as his eyes opened, he saw a swirl of crimson smoke had appeared in his darkened room. A sinister, scaly figure was sitting at its centre — a velociraptor with orange and black skin and pointed jaws that were scuffed and scraped. His right eye was covered by a patch, but the other gleamed with cunning.

Teggs stared in horror. "General Loki! *Here?*"

"Greetings, you stego-simpleton! I have come to haunt you from the realm of nightmares . . ." Slowly, magically, Loki rose into the smoky air. "Soon you and your crew will enter my deadly dream world," he snarled. "And when you do, you shall never get out again. You are doomed, Teggs. *DOOMED!*"

Chapter Three

WHERE HAVE ALL THE PTEROSAURS GONE?

Teggs glared at the figure floating before him. "Either I'm still dreaming, or this is a trick." He raised the club-like tip of his tail. "And I don't like being tricked – especially by rotten raptors!"

Loki just threw back his head and laughed. Teggs swung his tail through the air to strike him, but the bony spikes sliced through thin air. Loki had vanished.

Then, suddenly, the whole ship shook – and it started raining in Teggs's cabin!

"What the . . . ?" Cold water poured down on Teggs, jolting him properly awake. He looked up to find the sprinklers in the ceiling had come on. "It *must* have been a dream. But it seemed so real . . ." He frowned, shaking his head as the water droplets fell on him. "Hang on – there's no fire in here, and the alarm pterosaur isn't squawking. So what set off the sprinklers?" He looked at his clock. "Great galaxies, I've been asleep for five hours! Funny how time passes in a dream . . ."

Quickly changing into his slightly soggy red uniform, Teggs went into the corridor. The sprinklers were squirting out here too. In fact, water rained down on him all the way to the *Sauropod*'s main lift. Several of the crew were scrambling up sleepily from the wet floor.

Teggs raised his eyebrows. "When I offered everyone a rest break, I thought they might go to their rooms first!"

The lift doors opened – and there was Arx, blinking as if he had just woken up. "Hello, Captain," he said, rising stiffly to his feet. "Did you sleep well?"

"I certainly slept," Teggs agreed, entering the lift. "But I had odd dreams. One about bushes that bit back, and then one about General Loki. I felt like I could actually reach out and touch him . . ."

"Dreams often seem real," said Arx, yawning. "In mine, I was an astro-knight, with a jousting pole and everything!"

Teggs smiled. "That sounds like fun!"

They soon reached the flight deck, which was looking a bit tidier. Gipsy was still asleep by her controls. Teggs glanced up at the red crystal meteor poking through the roof, and sighed. Most of the sprinklers here had been destroyed, but one still worked, dripping water onto Gipsy's head. "Ugh!" she said, waking suddenly with a fright. "What a nasty nightmare. I dreamed I was being attacked by sabre-toothed bananas . . ."

Teggs and Arx stared at her. "Sabre-toothed bananas?" they echoed.

Gipsy's head-crest flushed purple, and she shrugged. "I can't help what I dream about!"

"Neither can I," said Iggy, breezing back in with an umbrella. "I always have the same dream about beating the raptors in a space-car race. Only this time I beat them on jet-cycles as well! Cool or what?"

"Never mind cool – it's downright cold with the sprinklers on!" said Teggs, pulling at his wet uniform. "What set them off?"

"I was about to ask the same thing," Iggy said, as Arx crossed to his controls. "And where have the dimorphodon gone?"

Teggs looked around the flight deck. There was not a pterosaur to be seen. "Perhaps they got tired after all. Give Sprite a call, Gipsy."

Gipsy switched on her communicator and gave a long whistle. She waited for a reply. But the loudspeakers stayed silent.

"Maybe they're just sleeping really deeply," suggested Iggy.

"Maybe." Teggs had an uneasy feeling. "But isn't it strange that everyone on board seems to have fallen asleep at the same time?"

"I've deactivated the sprinkler system," Arx announced, staring down at his controls. "Now I'll just check what caused the— Oh, *no!*" His horns drooped. "There's been a fire in the alarm-pterosaur's cabin!"

"What?" cried Teggs. "Is she OK?"

"I don't know . . ." Arx couldn't believe

his own instruments. "The fire was so intense it overloaded the sprinkler controls and set them off all over the ship! What could cause such a thing?"

Iggy scratched his head. "Whatever it was, I can't believe that we slept right through it!"

"Calling Terri Alarmosaurus!" said Gipsy urgently, broadcasting all over the ship. "Are you there, Terri? Squawk to us, please!" She frowned. "Perhaps Sprite and the other dimorphodon found out about the fire and rushed to her rescue?"

"Come on!" Teggs jumped into the lift. "Let's get down there and check everyone's OK . . ."

Gipsy, Arx and Iggy all bundled after him.

And as they left the flight deck, a deep crimson

glow began to pulse in the heart of the crystal meteor. Softly at first. But then, brighter . . .

The astrosaurs raced through the waterlogged corridors of level ten until they slipped and slid to a halt outside Terri's cabin. Foul-smelling smoke belched from inside. The fire had gone out, but the heat in the burned-out cabin was still enough to roast a giant turnip in seconds.

Normally, Teggs would have popped to the kitchens, taken several giant turnips and done exactly that. But right now, a terrible sadness had silenced his stomach. "Poor Terri," he whispered.

"Wait!" Arx pointed to a large, smeared mark in the soggy ash further along the corridor. "It looks a bit like a giant footprint. Perhaps something dragged Terri away."

"Let's see if we can find any more tracks," said Gipsy, splashing off down the corridor. But as she turned the corner she skidded to a stop, speechless with shock.

Three sleek and shiny space-cars were blocking her way – one red, one yellow, one blue. Their engines burst into growling, noisy life as they nudged forward, ready to run Gipsy down. And there, behind the steering wheel of each of the rocket-powered racers, sat a dribbling, deadly *RAPTOR!*

Chapter Four

THE NIGHTMARE CHASE

With the revving of engines loud in her ears, Gipsy sprinted back down the corridor towards her friends. "Look out!" she yelled. "Raptors!"

Teggs stared at her. "*What?*"

But already, the space-cars were scraping around the corner, their raptor drivers snarling.

please no running

"I . . . I don't believe it!" Iggy stammered. "The raptors, those space-cars . . . they're straight out of my dream!"

"Interesting coincidence, I'm sure," said Teggs. "Now, *RUN!*"

Luckily there wasn't quite room for all three space-cars to turn the corner at once. The raptors bumped into each other, each desperate to be first to reach the astrosaurs . . . giving Teggs and his friends precious seconds to charge away.

"I think we must *all* be dreaming," Arx panted. "How could raptors bring

space-cars on board the *Sauropod*?"

"They must have sneaked in while we were asleep," said Gipsy.

"And now they're going to run us down," Iggy puffed crossly. "Don't they know a collision could seriously damage the ship's bodywork?"

Gipsy frowned. "It won't do wonders for ours either!"

Teggs heard the roar of the space-cars growing louder behind him, sped up as he took the next corner – and with a mighty "*OOF!*" went crashing into something sleek and shiny-black . . .

"Captain!" Gipsy helped him up. "Are you all right?"

"I think so," said Teggs, staring at the obstacles in his way. "But this is getting crazier by the moment . . ."

"Three jet-cycles!" Arx declared. The powerful, dung-burning bikes were parked in a row, ready to mount. "But where did they come from?"

"From out of my dream, just like the raptors in the space-cars!" Iggy was grinning from ear to ear as he leaped into the saddle of the closest jet-cycle. "I don't know how they got here or what's going on, but jump on board,

guys – we'll outrun those raptors
for sure!"

"These contraptions simply *can't* have
appeared out of nowhere," Arx pointed
out sensibly, climbing onto the second
bike. "Even if you *did* dream about
them."

"I wouldn't be so sure, Arx." Teggs
helped Gipsy onto the third jet-
cycle then picked up something
long, sharp and silvery from
the floor. "Have you ever
seen this before?"

"It's a jousting
pole!" Arx gulped.
"Like the one
I used in
my dream,

when I was an astro-knight . . ."

Teggs nodded grimly. General Loki's ominous words echoed in his head: *Soon you and your crew will enter my deadly dream world*! "But that was just a nightmare," he muttered. "Wasn't it?"

Suddenly, the raptors came screeching round the corner in their brightly coloured space-cars, blocking each other's way again. They honked their horns, growling louder than their engines.

"Dream or not, it's time to motor,"

Iggy yelled. "Come on, Captain, I'll give you a backie!"

"No, you three get going while I hold off the raptors," Teggs commanded. "Get the main doors open – I'll meet you there."

As Gipsy, Arx and Iggy sped away, Teggs turned to face the space-cars with his jousting pole. Then he wedged the long, shiny pole between the walls of the corridor, blocking the way.

"That's what I call a finishing line!" said Teggs with satisfaction. As the space-cars revved their engines, he charged away up the corridor, galloping faster and faster . . .

At last, with a stitch in his side, Teggs reached the main doors. Arx, Gipsy and Iggy had already parked their jet-cycles and were banging helplessly on the stubborn steel shutters.

"Get those doors open!" said Teggs, breathlessly.

Iggy shook his head. "We can't, Captain."

"It's as if someone has blocked them from the outside," Arx revealed. "More raptors, perhaps?"

"But where did they come from? The sensors showed this planet was deserted, that no spaceships had come here . . ." Gipsy stamped her foot with frustration. "Nothing makes sense. It's like being stuck in some horrible nightmare!"

"*That's because you* are, *my dear!*" came a vile, villainous voice.

The astrosaurs whirled round, and Teggs felt a shiver run down his spiky back. A swirl of crimson smoke had formed behind them, just as it had in his cabin. And the same familiar, eye-patched figure sat hunched at its centre.

Arx gasped. "Loki!"

"I'm afraid I gummed up the door," rasped the black-and-orange raptor. "And then I used my short-range

teleport to get inside . . ."
Iggy lunged for him,
but Loki rose up
into the air, out
of reach. "Pardon
my smoke — it's
these anti-
gravity boots I'm
wearing, so none
of you can
reach me!"

"Coward,"
snarled Teggs.

"*Coward?*
Me?" The raptor looked appalled. "I'm
General Loki — commander of the Seven
Fleets of Death! Ruler of the meat mines
of Raptos! Attacker of apatosaurus, eater
of elfosaur—"

"Never mind all that nonsense," said
Teggs sternly. "What's happened to the
alarm pterosaur and my flight crew?"

Loki's one eye gleamed as he stared

down at them. "That is *my* business. You would do better to worry about your own situation, potato-pants." He laughed. "I control the meteors that attacked your ship – *living* meteors, filled with incredible energy."

"A raptor weapon, I suppose?" said Arx.

"One that gives me power over the world of dreams," Loki hissed. "First, my meteor in the flight deck sent everyone on this ship into a deep sleep. Then it looked into your heads and brought your dreams to life . . ." He rubbed his cruel claws together with glee. "And now those dream-creatures are coming to get you!"

Chapter Five

BANANAS OF DOOM

"Could it be true?" Teggs murmured.
"Good dreams and bad dreams, all
tangled up with real life . . ."

"It's true, all right," Loki gloated.
"The meteors' powers have plunged
you into a living nightmare – and

there is nowhere to
run!" He pointed
past the astrosaurs,
to where the raptors
had appeared
around the corner
in their red, blue
and yellow space-
cars. "See . . . ?"

"Quick, guys!" Teggs cried. "Get back on your jet-cycles."

"I think not, Captain . . ." Loki pointed a clawed finger, there was a flash of scarlet light – and the jet-cycles vanished!

Iggy gulped. "My dream bikes!"

"No, fool . . ." Loki snapped his long, pointed jaws. "*My* dream-bikes. The meteors have brought your dreams and nightmares to life, but I control them all!"

"Don't let him distract you, guys," Teggs told his friends. "If we can't drive off, we'll stand and fight."

"Not if I don't want you to!" Loki pointed his finger at the raptors in their space-cars – and in two more scarlet flashes, *they* disappeared too! "Nothing happens here unless I allow it . . ."

Gipsy stared at Loki in amazement. "You just destroyed your own raptors!"

He shrugged. "They were only dreams."

"Hang on a minute," cried Teggs. "Dreams aren't real – how can they hurt us?"

Loki gave him an unpleasant smile. "Allow me to demonstrate, pea-brain . . ."

"Captain!" Gipsy clutched his arm. "Look behind you!"

A large banana had appeared on the floor.

"Huh," said Teggs. "What's that going to do? Give me indigestion if I eat it?"

But suddenly, the banana jumped up and balanced on its stalk. A mouth opened up in the side of it to reveal two sharp yellow fangs . . .

"Captain, it's a sabre-toothed banana!"

Gipsy shouted, backing away in panic.
"Just like in my nightmare!"

Teggs tried to whack it away with his
tail – but the banana chomped down
on the tip! "*OW!*" yelled Teggs, trying to
shake it loose. "Get off!"

Arx and Iggy went to help him – but
more bananas rained down on their
heads! One of the fierce fruits unpeeled
itself a little and thwacked Gipsy on the
snout. "They always attack in bunches,"
she cried, as another banana bared its
fangs. "I dreamed them that way."

"You see, astro-fools?" Loki threw back his scaly, stripy head and laughed. "You *can* be hurt by these diabolical dream-demons. And you can be destroyed too – any time I choose . . ."

"Talk to the tail, Loki." Teggs punched another gnashing 'nana to the floor. "We've beaten you before, we can beat you again."

"Right!" cried Iggy. He punched a banana so hard that it disappeared with a fruity pop! "Hey, where'd it go?"

"I don't know." Arx stamped down hard on another banana – *POP!* "But this one went the same way."

"Cool!" Teggs curled up into a spiky ball and hurled himself about the corridor, bursting bananas with every bounce. "The harder you hit them, the faster they *split!*"

Gipsy tail-swiped the last banana standing and it popped out of existence. "So much for your deadly dreams, Loki!"

But the raptor general went on smiling. "I was about to say – to make things more fun, I've made some of the dream-creatures simple to deal with, while others are deadly at first touch." He leered down at them. "I do hope you'll enjoy discovering which is which . . ."

"Why all this game-playing, Loki?" Teggs demanded. "Just tell us where you've taken Terri and the dimorphodon, and what it is that you want!"

"You'll find out soon enough . . ." Loki began to fade away. "If you live that long!" His mocking laughter lingered in the air, even after the last wisp of scarlet smoke from his boots had vanished.

"Captain, what are we going to do?" asked Gipsy nervously.

"We must round up the crew and put them into teams," Teggs declared. "There's safety in numbers, and we must be ready to fight anything and everything."

"Of course." Iggy swallowed hard. "So far we've only had things from our own dreams to deal with. But with so many other astrosaurs on board, there will be *loads* of nightmare creatures stomping about!"

"Maybe we'll only meet the ones that are easy to destroy," said Arx brightly.

Gipsy sighed. "Or maybe we won't."

Suddenly, a loud *thump* echoed from round the corner. It sounded like a huge sack of slime had been thrown to the floor. *THUMP!* There it was again, louder this time, followed by a throaty, bad-tempered roar . . .

"Wait a moment." Teggs narrowed his eyes as the loudest **THUMP** yet shook the floor. "I've heard that sound somewhere before."

"So have I." Iggy gasped. "It was back on the planet Creepus . . ."

"Oh, no!" Teggs looked at him in alarm. "Don't tell me someone has dreamed about *that* thing . . ."

"What thing?" asked Gipsy, puzzled.

She had her answer a moment later as a horrifying monster hopped into sight. It was a huge, red spiky ball with a gaping mouth crammed with white jagged teeth. A big, pink muscly arm, ending in a fist, sprouted from its top. The monster had just one phenomenal foot, with sixteen spindly toes. And

on the end of every toe there was a bloodshot red eyeball, staring around with hatred.

"Bless my horns!" cried Arx. "What is that brute?"

"Loki's pet," said Teggs grimly. "It's a kraggle-scruncher – one of the deadliest creatures in the universe!"

Chapter Six

HORRORS OF THE MIND

The bizarre monster growled menacingly.

Arx shuddered. "He looks tougher than the bananas."

Gipsy stared at the monster's massive foot. "So *that*'s what made the print we found on the floor outside Terri's cabin."

Teggs nodded. "It explains the fire there too."

Arx frowned. "It does?"

Suddenly, the kraggle-scruncher spat a blistering ball of white flame straight at the astrosaurs!

"See what I mean?" Desperately, Teggs shoved his friends aside. The fireball blazed past – missing the gang

by millimetres – and scorched the wall behind them. "Now, run!"

The astrosaurs sprinted away like contestants in the Great Dinosaur Games. They dashed down dozens of corridors. Along one, they found a cleaner being threatened by a bunch of snarling bushes from Teggs's dream. Iggy jumped up and down on the bushes until they popped, and Gipsy hid the cleaner in a cupboard.

"Can't we hide with her, till the kraggle-scruncher goes past?" Arx panted.

"Not a chance," said Teggs. "Now it's got our scent, it'll never stop hunting us!"

THUMP! THUMP! THUMP! went the kraggle-scruncher behind them.

The astrosaurs sped off again – straight into the path of a humungous mop, and a sponge the size of a bus! "Ooof!" Teggs yelled as the mop's white raggedy end knocked him aside. The sponge splashed him with water, and then both objects whizzed away out of sight.

Iggy helped Teggs to his feet. "I wonder if that cleaner dreamed up those things?"

Teggs nodded gravely. "I wonder what else we will bump into . . ."

The kraggle-scruncher roared in the distance, and the astrosaurs ran off yet again. But the dream-things seemed determined to slow them down. A fierce flock of butterflies made of newspaper flapped into their faces. A spotty pink squid tried to trip them with its tentacles. They even had to pick their way through a dense forest made out of smelly cheese.

"How can so many weird and wonderful things suddenly come to life like this?" Gipsy groaned. "Those meteors really must be magic!"

"I don't understand how Loki took control of them so fast," said Arx. "He's only been out of prison for a few days. And how did he get here without a spaceship?"

"However he managed it, he's more powerful than ever." Iggy swatted at a flying pink scorpion as they pushed through the last of the cheesy trees. "He's playing with us!"

"We mustn't give up," Teggs told his friends, leading them up the steps to level nine and setting off again along the corridor. But as they rounded a corner, they almost crashed into two ankylosaur guards charging the other way. Just behind them was their spiky security chief, Alass.

"Captain, what's happening?" she wailed. "It's like we're caught up in some demented dream!"

"Actually, demented dreams are catching up with *us*!" Teggs corrected her. "Thanks to General Loki."

"We've been going round the ship telling everyone to hide in their rooms," she went on. "But now there's something nasty on our trail."

"What is it?" Iggy asked. "Raptors? Bananas?"

Alass shook her head with a fearful look in her eyes. "Dung!"

The next moment, an enormous ball of squishy, quivering dung squelched into sight! Its black-and-brown bulk filled the corridor from floor to ceiling, and its stink poisoned the air.

"Great galaxies!" Teggs clutched his throat. "Who in the world would ever dream of something like that?"

One of the guards blushed and
sheepishly put up his claw.

Without warning, the dung-monster
spat a huge pile of steaming dung at Arx
and Gipsy. They jumped aside just in
time.

"Perhaps it's another easy-to-pop
monster," said Iggy hopefully. He swiped
it with his tail – which came out covered
with steaming, stinky sludge. "Ugh!"

"Nice try." Teggs pulled Iggy away.

"But that thing is too big to bash."

"It will smother us all," Gipsy groaned.
"There's no way past!"

THUMP! THUMP! They could hear
the kraggle-scruncher hopping up the
stairs behind them.

SQUEEEELLLCH! Ahead of them,
the deadly dung-ball rolled closer.

"Uh-oh!" Arx swallowed hard. "Now
we're trapped!"

Just then, the giant, flying mop came
whizzing back, homing in on the
astrosaurs. "Oi!" Iggy ducked aside and
grabbed hold of it crossly. "As if we didn't
have enough problems!"

"Hang on, Iggy," said Teggs, helping
him hold onto the marauding mop. "This
could be just what we need!"

Gipsy looked puzzled. "Even a *giant* mop
is no good against that dung-demon."

"True," said Teggs. "But it's raising our
chances of survival through the *roof*!"
Twisting hard, he jammed the mop-head

against the ceiling of the corridor, and then wedged the end of its handle into the floor. "Hey, presto! Instant fire-fighter's pole – only this one we'll have to slide up. That's not just the ceiling of level nine above us; it's the floor of level eight. We must try to break through."

"Allow me!" Iggy was already shinning up the pole with an astro-wrench snatched from his tool kit. "There's an inspection hatch up here . . ." He quickly fiddled with several bolts in the ceiling until they fell away – quickly followed by a large metal panel that clattered to the floor.

"You did it!" cried Gipsy, as the dung-ball slithered still closer.

Iggy kissed his astro-wrench. "Now, if I can just loosen the floor panel above . . ."

But suddenly, the kraggle-scruncher bounced into view. At the sight of the astrosaurs in front of it, all sixteen of its pink eyes narrowed with hatred.

"Quickly, everyone!" cried Teggs. "Climb up there and help Iggy!"

Gipsy and Alass were up the mop-handle first, banging on the stubborn panel. Arx squeezed up too and tried to prise it free with his horns. The guards rushed at the kraggle-scruncher but it punched one guard senseless and kicked the other into the wall.

"It's no good!" Gipsy shook her aching hoofs. "We can't break through."

"But you must!" Teggs shouted, as the kraggle-scruncher hopped closer and the dung-monster moved in for the kill. "You *MUST*!"

Chapter Seven

RAPTOR REALITY

In desperation, Teggs hurled the inspection hatch at the kraggle-scruncher. But the beast batted it away and opened its mouth. A fireball formed there and the

creature got ready to roast the astrosaurs alive . . .

Just as the giant dung-ball spat an enormous mound of manure at the one-footed fury – burying it completely!

Teggs smiled grimly. "That thing doesn't distinguish between dinosaurs and alien weirdoes – it wants to get *everyone*!"

The kraggle-scruncher broke free and started bouncing off the walls, howling mad and scattering muck everywhere.

Iggy finally flipped up the floor panel. "Come on, you lot! We're through to level eight!"

"Quick!" Teggs hissed, helping the dazed ankylosaur guards climb the mop handle. Then

61

he shinned up to safety himself — as the kraggle-scruncher shook off the last of the manure and launched a fearsome fireball at the dung-ball in its path!

A deafening *POP!* echoed from the corridor below.

Arx peeped back through the hole and saw that the devilish dung-ball was gone, destroyed by the kraggle-scruncher's fiery attack. But unlike the other dream things, it hadn't disappeared completely.

From up here, Arx could see tiny gleaming shards of red crystal, scattered all over the floor below. "That's interesting," he murmured, "very interesting . . ."

The kraggle-scruncher grabbed hold of the mop with its one enormous hand and started to pull itself up after the astrosaurs. Arx rolled backwards as the creature sent a blast of fire bursting up through the hole – and in the fierce white light, the triceratops saw something sparkling on Teggs's back.

"Aha!" Arx hurried over to take a closer look. "Just as I thought." He gazed round excitedly at the others. "I think I know the secret of the dream-demons. But to prove my theory, we must capture the kraggle-scruncher!"

Gipsy stared at him. "Capture it? How?"

The kraggle-scruncher roared. A huge pink palm slapped down on the deck as it started to pull itself through the hole. The astrosaurs backed quickly away.

"I have an idea that might work," Iggy murmured. "But we'll need to go to the engine room!"

"So what are we waiting for?" Teggs gave Iggy a crooked smile and sprinted away. "Let's do it!"

There was another bunch of savage,

sabre-toothed bananas lurking outside the engine room. Teggs whacked one with his tail – but this time, it didn't go pop. Instead, it jumped up at his tummy and sank its fruity fangs into his flesh with fearsome force. "Ow!" Teggs yelled. "These things are tougher than before!"

"They certainly are!" Gipsy wrenched the savage fruit away, but it wriggled out of her grip and attacked her. Alass grabbed the banana in mid-air and hurled it away, while her guards swept aside the others with their bony, club-like tails.

Iggy led everyone into the engine room and they closed the doors behind them. It was a large rectangular space that housed not only the *Sauropod*'s mighty motors but also the dung-burners – clever machines that turned raw dung into fuel.

"I wasn't expecting those bananas to

be so hard to get rid of," Arx admitted.

"We've been chasing about the ship for three hours," Iggy reminded him. "We're probably just tired."

"It's more than that." Arx scratched his horns. "It's almost as if the dream-demons are getting stronger as time goes by . . ."

"All the more reason why we must catch that kraggle-scruncher, and fast," said Teggs. "What's your plan, Ig?"

"It's a bit dodgy," Iggy admitted. "But

if we can get the kraggle-scruncher to shoot a close-range fireball at the dung-burners, it'll cause an explosion that should stop it in its tracks."

"And then we can capture it!" Teggs beamed.

"Perhaps it'll just go pop?" said Gipsy hopefully.

"Actually," said Arx, "I don't think the kraggle-scruncher can ever go pop . . ."

Before anyone could ask what he meant, a familiar cloud of crimson smoke appeared at the far end of the engine room, the shadowy outline of a raptor forming at its centre. Alass and the ankylosaurs gasped.

"It's all right," Teggs told them. "It's only Loki, back to bug us."

"And look," said Gipsy, "he's holding something in his claw . . ."

Teggs bunched his fists. "It's the alarm pterosaur!"

Sure enough, Loki was holding poor Terri by the throat. "Don't you dare damage this ship's engines, astro-fools!" he growled, bobbing about in the smoky air. "If you do – I'll squish this dainty dino-bird."

The alarm pterosaur stretched out to Teggs feebly with her wings.

"Put her down!" Teggs shouted. "What do you care about our engines, anyway?"

"Because the *Sauropod* will soon be mine," Loki snarled. "And I've got quite enough repairs to make to it already!"

Through the door, the astrosaurs heard the approaching step of the tireless

kraggle-scruncher. *Thump. THUMP!*
THUMP! The beat of the monster's footsteps quickened, like the pounding of a heart.

Loki swung his tail gleefully and Terri choked on a wisp of scarlet smoke. "My little pet is coming for you."

Iggy looked at Teggs. "If we can't stop it with the dung-burners, it'll destroy us all."

Teggs nodded. "But if we *do* stop it, Loki will squish poor Terri!"

"Precisely!" Loki's one staring eye was bright with menace. "You have served your purpose, plant-eaters. I no longer need you. But I *do* need your ship, and your precious undreaming pterosaurs to fly it for me – that's why I stole them all away . . ."

The kraggle-scruncher started banging on the engine-room door.

"Captain," Gipsy cried, "what can we do?"

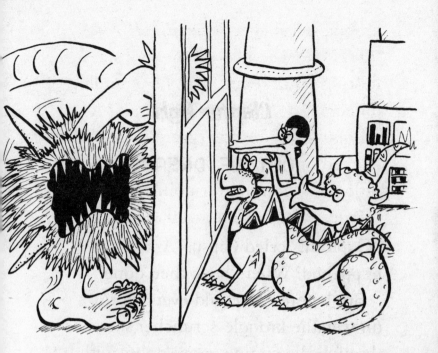

"We must beg Loki for mercy," said
Teggs, padding over to the floating
raptor, his head bowed. "Either that
or . . . *ATTACK!*"

"No!" Loki gasped, as Teggs sprung
furiously towards him. Something fell
from the raptor's free hand. The smoke
engulfed Loki, Teggs, and Terri, too . . .

When it faded, all three had vanished!

Chapter Eight

OUT OF DREAMS

"Captain!" cried Gipsy. "Arx, what happened? Where have they gone?"

But before Arx could even try to answer, the kraggle-scruncher smashed through the engine-room doors with a horrible howl.

Bravely, Iggy ran up to the monster and stamped on its foot. The kraggle-scruncher knocked him to the floor and opened its snarling, awful mouth to unleash a fireball . . .

Then Alass and her guards ran up behind it and butted it as hard as they could. The kraggle-scruncher tripped over Iggy and its flame struck the dung-burners . . .

"Oh, no!" wailed Gipsy.

"Down, everyone!" Arx yelled.

KER-KRUMMP! The dung-burner
blew up with a smoky, smelly explosion.
The kraggle-scruncher was thrown
against the far wall and landed in
a heap.

"We didn't mean to damage the
engine!" said Alass in alarm. "Loki won't
really hurt Terri, will he?"

"He will need her to help fly the ship,"

Arx muttered, studying their fallen foe.
"Besides, I'm sure Captain Teggs won't
let any harm come to Terri, wherever
they've gone."

"I hope they're all right," said Gipsy
sadly. "How's the kraggle-scruncher?"

"Arx was right, it
didn't go pop." Iggy
rubbed his bruised
jaw. "Just how tough
is that dream-thing?"

"The kraggle-
scruncher is a *living*
thing – not a dream-
demon at all!" Arx
told them, examining the monster. "Yes,
it's got a pulse in its foot . . . and two
hearts beating in its arm. We knocked it
out, that's all." Suddenly, a sabre-toothed
banana bounced into the room, and Arx
grabbed it. "You see, dream-things like
this one are quite different. They have no
heartbeat or pulse at all."

"Because they are magic dream-monsters?" asked Alass.

"No, because they are made of meteor crystals!" Arx declared. "Crystals with the power to take any shape and texture they choose."

Gipsy stared at him in amazement. "You said those meteors contained some kind of strange energy . . ."

Iggy nodded. "And Loki said they were a raptor weapon."

"A very advanced one too," Arx agreed. "You know how an astro-camera takes snapshots of space that we then print on special paper? Well, I think that the meteor on the flight deck took snapshots of our dreams, printed them onto special crystals – and then sent them to get us . . ." He squeezed the banana with all his strength, and finally it vanished with a pop. "See?"

Gipsy peered closely at his hands and saw they were covered in tiny fragments

73

of red crystal. "So, we've been fighting crystal reproductions of our dreams!" she breathed. "No wonder they shattered when we hit them hard enough."

"I only noticed when the kraggle-scruncher destroyed that giant dung-ball," Arx admitted. "It was *so* big that the crystal fragments it left behind were easy to spot. Then I noticed tiny bits of crystal on the captain's back where he squashed those dream-bananas."

"But how did Loki make those space-cars disappear just by pointing at them?" asked Iggy.

"I wonder . . ." Arx bounded over to where Loki had appeared, and picked up a small metal device from the floor. "Aha! The general dropped this when Captain Teggs jumped him. It looks like a miniature light-cannon . . ." Another sabre-toothed banana bounced obligingly into the room, and Arx quickly squeezed a button on the gadget.

There was a flash of light, and the banana burst into tiny tell-tale splinters. "There you go. Loki used *this* to get rid of the meteor's projections."

One of the ankylosaur guards was scratching his head with his tail. "But why would Loki send a real kraggle-scruncher after us as well as the dream-demons?"

"Perhaps the dream-demons weren't quite ready to fight," Iggy suggested. "We all woke up when the kraggle-scruncher's fire set off the sprinklers by accident, right? Maybe we were *supposed* to stay sleeping for a few hours longer . . ."

"The bananas have certainly got stronger as time's gone by," Gipsy agreed. "I bet you're right, Ig – Loki tricked us with a real kraggle-scruncher so we wouldn't guess how weak the dream-demons were back then!"

"We messed up our best chance to fight back!" said Arx grimly. "I only wish

we knew where Loki has gone now with
the captain and Terri."

Gipsy sighed. "*I* only wish we knew
what to do next."

"That one's easy," growled Alass.
"However tough these dream-things are,
we must reach that miserable meteor on
the flight deck – and *SMASH* it!"

Teggs woke with a groan somewhere
dark and cold. After grabbing hold of
Loki, the world had started to spin.
He'd felt himself fading away, and then
growing solid again somewhere else.
How long had he been asleep – seconds?
Hours?

"Loki!" he shouted. "Where are you?"
He choked on smoke seeping from Loki's
discarded anti-gravity boots, lying on the
ground. "What have you done with my
alarm pterosaur?"

A dim light shone to the left of him
through a crimson haze. Teggs staggered

towards it in the hope of finding fresh air – and found himself in the mouth of a massive cave. Gulping down deep breaths, he saw another large red crystal, like the one stuck in the roof of the *Sauropod*, hooked up to a strange machine with dozens of smaller crystals scattered around it. Each of the red stones showed a different view of the *Sauropod*'s decks and corridors. In one of them, he saw a cleaner fending off a flying scorpion. In another, an engineer was running from a giant egg.

"Loki's been spying on us," Teggs murmured angrily. "Watching as we've been fighting those dream-demons." Then, with a thrill of delight, he noticed that one crystal showed Arx, Gipsy, Iggy and the others standing over the body of the kraggle-scruncher. "We've beaten your big-footed friend, Loki!" he shouted. "Now, where are you? And where am I, for that matter?"

Outside the cave, an alien sun was shining in the hazy blue sky. Teggs crossed to the cave mouth – and there, across the barren plains before him, was the *Sauropod*! The huge crimson meteor that crowned its crumpled top was sparkling in the sunlight like an enormous exotic jewel.

"So, I'm outside on Mallakar," Teggs realized.

"And here you shall perish, you sludge-brained stegosaurus!"

At the sound of Loki's slightly muffled voice, Teggs whirled round to face the shadows. "Come out, Loki," he ordered. "I know you've been teleporting in and out of my ship from here. Just come out and face me, dinosaur to dinosaur."

"Very well . . ." A mechanical crunching noise carried from the back of the cave – followed by the whirring of engines. "Here I am!"

Teggs gasped as a strange metal sculpture came floating towards him. It looked like an armoured spacesuit built for a kraggle-scruncher, with various weapons attached to the oversized foot. Crimson anti-gravity vapour swirled from its metal sole. A large glass box was balanced on top of the arm where the fist should have been.

And there inside the box, steering the suit with huge switches, was General Loki. "That's right, Captain," he snarled. "This is where your nightmares *really* begin!"

80

Chapter Nine

THE CHAOS AND THE CRYSTAL

"So that's how you escaped from space prison," Teggs realized. "And why Arx found no trace of a spaceship on Mallakar. That kraggle-scruncher of yours sneaked under the DSS radar in a jet-propelled armoured spacesuit and carried you away!"

"It was sent to release me by the Raptor Royal himself!" said Loki proudly, floating a little higher into the air. "He needed someone he could trust to test out our mighty meteors. And since I knew you leaf-nibbling fools would be chasing after me, I decided to test them on *YOU*! But it takes at least eight hours for the dream-demons to reach maximum strength, and you awoke after only five . . ."

"So you kept us busy with your kraggle-scruncher until they were properly cooked." Teggs scowled. "But never mind that. What have you done with Terri Alarmosaurus?"

"I stuck that dreary dino-bird back in her cage." Loki smiled down from his box. "You would do better to worry about your own safety . . ." As he spoke, he stamped down at Teggs with the great iron foot of his borrowed suit. Caught off-guard, the captain barely jumped clear in time. "Once your crew see that I've crushed you, they will soon surrender your ship!"

Teggs scrambled to his feet. "Why do you need the *Sauropod*, anyway?"

"To deliver the dream-meteors all around the Vegetarian Sector!" Loki grinned as his suit rose back up into the air. "They can move through space by themselves, of course – how else could we have steered them here from Raptos? – but they are somewhat slow." He tried to stamp on Teggs again, narrowly missing the stegosaur's tail. "And, in order to cause maximum damage in the shortest possible time, I need a super-fast spaceship that can deliver the meteors to any plant-eater planet or DSS space station without arousing suspicion."

"Of course," Teggs realized grimly. "The *Sauropod* has a licence to travel anywhere."

"The meteors will force entire populations to fall asleep," hissed Loki. "And when the plant-eaters wake up they will find that their dreams and nightmares have come to terrible life . . ."

"While raptor spaceships sneak into orbit, ready to attack once the chaos is underway." Teggs shivered. "You'll be able to conquer whole planets overnight."

Loki was exultant. "Precisely!"

Suddenly, Teggs caught movement in the cave behind Loki. It was Sprite!

Somehow, he had gotten free. Now he looked at Teggs and whirled his wing around. The message was clear – *keep Loki talking*. Then the dimorphodon dipped back inside the cave.

"You won't succeed, you know, Loki." Teggs raised his voice, so that Sprite could hear him. "I'll bet that even now, my plucky crew are working out a way to get to the flight deck and destroy your mouldy meteor – and then they'll come for *you*!"

"As if!" snarled Loki. He flicked some switches, and the suit lunged towards Teggs once more.

Only this time, Teggs wasn't quite fast enough to avoid it. The iron boot kicked him through the air like a big, scaly football, and he landed on his belly in a daze.

"Get up, Teggs! Get up so I can kick you down again!" Loki was dancing around inside his glass box. "This mission will be my greatest triumph – Teggs Stegosaur squashed beneath my foot, while his precious Vegetarian Sector is left in tatters!"

Iggy, Alass and her two guards were fighting their way through the *Sauropod*'s corridors, heading for the flight deck. Arx and Gipsy were protecting them from the rear with the help of other astrosaurs they had picked up on the way.

Cleaners, engineers – even the small dinosaur in charge of making swamp-tea – they were all joining the fight against the weird crystal creations. Sabre-toothed bananas, T. rexes with ten tails, mosquitoes as big as a bear . . . the closer the crew got to the mysterious meteor, the more menaces popped up to get them.

"We're nearly through to the lift!" Iggy called. A bush with teeth was biting his foot, and another was chomping at

his tail. Alass kicked them away, as a swamp-snake in a ball gown tried to crush her ribs. "Then it's just a short trip up to the flight deck."

"But these things never seem to get tired," gasped Alass, wriggling free of the snake. "I don't think I can stand much more!"

"Hang on in there!" Arx urged her. He blasted a flying shark with Loki's light-cannon and it vanished with a *POP!* "We'll stop this meteor madness, you'll see!"

They managed to reach the lift and open the doors. A large swarm of small, winged mammoths holding mini cement shooters flew out from inside. The astrosaurs swatted them desperately as blobs of cement whizzed through the air.

Then Arx took Gipsy by the hoof and pulled her into the lift. Iggy jumped in and joined them. "Try not to let anything past you," Iggy told Alass. "We don't want any nasty surprises coming up behind us when we're trying to sort out that big meteor!"

Alass saluted, and the lift doors slid closed. Arx pressed the button that took them to the flight deck and the lift rose smoothly. The three astrosaurs swapped nervous looks.

As the doors opened, a red glare dazzled their eyes. The meteor was blazing with eerie light, pulsing with power. The sealing foam around it in the ruined roof had burned away, revealing glimpses of blue sky above.

But no dream-creatures appeared to attack them.

"This must be the eye of the storm," Arx murmured.

"You know . . ." Iggy yawned. "I'm starting to feel sleepy."

"It must be the power of the crystal," said Gipsy, her eyes drooping in the ghastly red glow. "Quickly, Arx. Zap it!"

"Here goes . . . !" He pointed the light-cannon and fired . . .

Nothing happened.

"Try again!" Gipsy urged him.

"Uh-oh," said Arx, tapping the cannon. "I must have used up too much power fighting the projections downstairs."

Iggy sank to his knees. "Must rest . . ."

"No, Iggy!" Arx shook the iguanodon awake – as the lift doors opened behind them.

There – burned and bruised and literally hopping mad – was the kraggle-scruncher!

"Oh, no!" Iggy's eyes widened.

Gipsy's head-crest turned bright blue. "It must have woken up!"

"And smashed its way past Alass and the others." Arx stood in front of her and Iggy protectively. "Now it's here to get us – once and for all."

With a bellow of rage, the kraggle-scruncher hopped into the flight deck, its fist clenched and ready to strike . . .

Chapter Ten

DREAM ON!

The kraggle-scruncher grabbed Arx and hurled him into Gipsy and Iggy. The three astrosaurs stared helplessly as the terrifying monster loomed over them . . .

When suddenly, something scaly and green zoomed down through a hole in the roof.

It was Sprite! He pecked the kraggle-scruncher on its biggest toe. The monster roared, blinking furiously, and tried to swat the dino-bird. But Sprite flew away just in time, and the 'scruncher gave himself eight black eyes.

"Sprite!" Gipsy beamed. "Where did you flap from?"

The dimorphodon landed on her
hoof. "Eep!"

"What?" she said, startled. "Loki locked
you and the other pterosaurs up in a
cave but you managed to untie your
wings, and when he grabbed Terri to
use as a hostage you secretly sneaked
out – and then Captain Teggs sent you
here to help us?"

Sprite nodded proudly.

"Er, guys?" Iggy interrupted. "I don't

think the meteor is very happy!"

Sure enough, the crystal's ruby-red glare was growing brighter, pulsing faster and faster.

"It knows it can't affect Sprite because pterosaurs can't dream," Arx realized. "And now it can't put us to sleep without putting the kraggle-scruncher to sleep as well!"

The kraggle-scruncher spat out a flesh-roasting fireball that missed Iggy by a whisker. But then Sprite whistled and suddenly a flock of dimorphodon came swooping down from the skies above.

"Yay!" Gipsy cheered. "Sprite set the others free too!"

The flight deck was plunged into fresh pandemonium. The dimorphodon flapped about, pecking the kraggle-scruncher all over. Arx and Iggy waded in and tried to wrestle its arm to the ground. The crystal throbbed angrily.

A fresh batch of sabre-toothed bananas
burst out of the lift, bouncing and biting
and adding to the confusion. Gipsy
kicked and punched them, but for every
one she knocked away, a dozen more
quickly appeared.

Then suddenly, the kraggle-scruncher
gave a deafening shriek and shook
off its attackers. Sprite whistled to the
dimorphodon and they regrouped in
tight formation – right in front of the
maddened, big-mouthed monster . . .

★ ★ ★

Outside the cave, Teggs was still desperately dodging Loki's enormous boot. He was exhausted and covered in mud, while Loki was cool and relaxed in his floating metal suit. *How much longer could he go on?*

Finally, Teggs slipped and bumped his head on a rock. He gasped with pain, helpless as Loki closed in for the kill.

"Your struggles no longer amuse me." Loki pulled a lever, and lethal-looking laser-guns poked out from the suit's metal toes. "Farewell, Teggs – it is

time to *DIE*!"

Teggs thought of his brave, loyal friends and closed his eyes. "Sorry, guys," he murmured, bracing himself for the blast.

But then a sudden flurry of stones came crashing down from on high between him and the laser-light, deflecting the deadly blast.

"Who dares to interfere?" Loki snarled.

Teggs looked up and beamed at the familiar figures dancing in the sky, several still clutching rocks in their claws. "My alarm pterosaur dares!"

he cried, "along with about a dozen dimorphodon, by the look of things!"

"*SQUAWK!*" said Terri, with a wink at her captain. Then she hurled another stone down at Loki in the kraggle-scruncher's spacesuit. The other dimorphodon joined in.

"Feeble fools!" Loki jeered. "Is that the best you can do?"

"As a distraction tactic, it works for me!" Teggs charged at Loki. "They've bought me time to do the best that *I* can do . . . *THIS!*"

Leaping through the air, Teggs struck Loki's protective suit with all four feet at once. The metal dented, the glass box shattered and the controls sparked and smoked. Loki squealed in alarm.

"Got you!" Teggs cried, reaching in to grab him.

"Wrong!" Loki snapped. "I have got you!" He jabbed two bare wires against Teggs's scaly skin, causing an electric shock that threw the stegosaur backwards, his head spinning as Terri's squawks of dismay and Loki's wild laughter echoed in his ears . . .

"Get back!" Gipsy yelled at the dimorphodon, who were hovering mere metres from the kraggle-scruncher's spiky mouth. "You won't stand a chance . . ."

But as the big beast blew out a truly enormous fireball, the pterosaurs dodged and scattered skywards – and the bundle of flame struck the crystal meteor in the roof instead!

Ka-BOOOOM! The meteor cracked open and exploded. The bouncing bananas went *POP!* Luminous fragments flew through the air as though a giant ruby chandelier had just shattered. Larger chunks of crystal rained down too, some as big as boulders. Iggy, Arx and Gipsy took shelter under their controls . . .

And once the downpour had stopped, Gipsy peered out to see what had become of the kraggle-scruncher. All that remained was a large, limp hand pointing up from a pile of red rubble.

"Good riddance to it," said Iggy. "*And* the meteor."

"They've gone!" Alass's shout of triumph carried up the lift shaft from the floor below, soon joined by the sound of applauding astrosaurs. "The dream-things have all gone!"

"And we're fine!" Iggy yelled down to her. "Result!"

"But where's the Captain, Sprite?" Arx looked worried. "And Terri – and Loki?"

102

"*Cherp!*" Sprite was already directing dimorphodon to lift one of the chunks of crystal, up into the air and out through the roof.

Gipsy's head-crest flushed blue again. "He says the captain's fighting for his life and we must all hurry to help him. Come on!"

Loki's gloating laughter was soon drowned out by the thundering explosion from the *Sauropod* – and replaced by the victorious squawks of Terri and the dimorphodon.

Still dazed from his electric shock, Teggs turned, in time to see the giant crystal meteor on top of his ship crack and tumble into pieces. "Yes!" he yelled.

"NO!" Loki screeched. "My crystal!"

"Looks like your dream world has come crashing down." Teggs struggled up. "Thanks to my fabulous friends!"

Teggs's crew were flying here from the *Sauropod* even now – with several dynamic dimorphodon carrying Arx, Iggy and Gipsy through the air between them. Sprite was carrying something else – a chunk of meteor . . .

"I still have my kraggle-scruncher," Loki growled. "He'll squash you all."

"Afraid not!" Iggy shouted down from the sky. "He got squashed when he accidentally blew up your rubbish rock!"

"No! I won't be beaten again!" Loki wailed. "The Raptor Royal won't give me another chance . . ." He jumped back into his broken box and started fiddling with the controls. "I can repair this. I'll

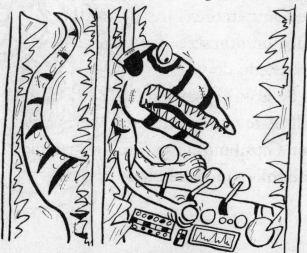

squish you all . . ."

"Dream on, Loki!" said Teggs. He gave Sprite the signal to drop the rock – right on the raptor general's head!

"*Urk!*" said Loki, as the rock bounced off his stripy skull. He dizzily closed his eyes, and flopped onto his back.

"Sweet dreams!" cried Arx, as the dimorphodon set him gently down beside Loki's sprawled body. A few moments later, Gipsy and Iggy were safely delivered too.

All three astrosaurs saluted their captain as the pterosaurs flapped joyfully above them through the skies of Mallakar.

Teggs saluted them back – then launched into a wild victory dance. Gipsy laughed and joined in, and so did Arx and Iggy.

"Isn't it just a dream come true to have woken up from this nightmare?" Teggs cried.

"We'll have to stay up for several nights to get the *Sauropod* fixed," said Arx.

"We'll make it better than ever," Iggy declared. "But what about the other dream-meteors still floating out there in space?"

"We'll get weapons experts from DSS HQ to gather them all up," said Arx. "They'll drop them into a black hole, where they can't bother anyone again."

Iggy glowered down at Loki. "I wish we could drop *him* into it too!"

"We'll take him straight back to space

prison," said Teggs, "don't you worry."

"I hope they guard him with nothing but pterosaurs, to remind him why he lost," said Arx mischievously. "In fact, I bet he's dreaming about Sprite and Terri right now!"

"As for you . . ." Gipsy nudged her captain in the ribs. "I bet you're already dreaming about another adventure, aren't you, sir?"

"Not me, Gipsy," Teggs declared with a smile. "Because, with a ship like the *Sauropod*, and you lot to help me fly it, I'm already *living* the dream – eight days a week!"

THE END

The **Astrosaurs** will return in
THE ROBOT RAIDERS

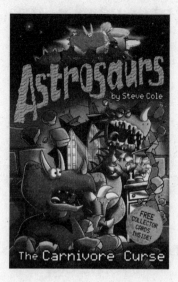

THE CARNIVORE CURSE
by Steve Cole

Teggs is no ordinary dinosaur – he's an ASROSAUR!
Captain of the amazing spaceship DSS *Sauropod*, he
goes on dangerous missions and fights evil – along
with his faithful crew, Gipsy, Arx and Iggy!

Teggs's new mission is to save a carnivore king from
deadly space mumps. If the king can't be cured, his evil
nephew will start a terrible war! The astrosaurs race to
the rescue with a special doctor – but are soon trapped
in a palace of peril. With enemies all around and
a mad meat-chomping monster on the loose, can
Teggs escape the heart-stopping horror of the
Carnivore Curse?

ISBN: 978 1 862 30256 3

MEET THE COWS IN ACTION!

THE TER-MOO-NATORS
by Steve Cole

IT'S 'UDDER' MADNESS!

Genius cow Professor McMoo and his trusty sidekicks,
Pat and Bo, are the star agents of the C.I.A. – short
for COWS IN ACTION! They travel through time,
fighting evil bulls from the future and keeping history
on the right track . . .

When Professor McMoo invents a brilliant TIME
MACHINE, he and his friends are soon attacked by
a terrifying TER-MOO-NATOR – a deadly robo-
cow who wants to mess with the past and change
the future! And that's only the start of an incredible
ADVENTURE that takes McMoo, Pat and Bo from a
cow paradise in the future to the SCARY dungeons of
King Henry VIII . . .

It's time for action. COWS IN ACTION

ISBN: 978 1 862 30189 4